D0418837
£3.25

The original Flower Fairies illustrations are
© The Estate of Cicely M. Barker, 1926, 1940, 1944.
The Annual is based on the Flower Fairies books
published by Blackie & Son Ltd., London and Glasgow.
Dolls photographs by kind permission of
Hornby Hobbies Limited.

Photography by *David Watts*, Thomas Neile Ltd.

The stories *The Narcissus Fairy*, *The Rose Fairy and The Midsummer Ball*, *The Hazelnut Fairy and The Elves*, *The Christmas Tree Fairy*; the features *A Pond in Spring*, *A Garden in Summer*, *A Hedgerow in September*, *A Wood in Winter*, were written by and are copyright *Rose Headland*.

Edited by
Rosemary Lanning.

Published by
GRANDREAMS LIMITED,
Jadwin House, 205/211 Kentish Town Road,
London NW5 2JU.

Printed in Holland.

ISBN 0 86227 333 1

Fixed price! £1.50

CONTENTS

Spring

The Narcissus Fairy

In a garden not far from where you live is a shady hollow with a small, round pool, and every spring the still water of the pool reflects a lovely picture — hundreds of yellow and white narcissus flowers, gently nodding when a breeze passes by.

In a secret corner of the hollow, which no human eyes have ever seen, is the home of the Narcissus Fairy. It is she who watches over the lovely flowers. She nurses them tenderly when rough March winds have jostled them and battered their pretty petals, and she guards them against greedy slugs and all other enemies. Each morning, at sunrise, while the family who own the garden are still fast asleep, she flies from flower to flower, bathing them in dewdrops and adding to each one a delicate scent.

Like all of the Flower Fairies, the Narcissus Fairy is very beautiful. She has long golden hair and wears the prettiest dress, with a silken skirt shaped just like the petals of her own special flowers.

Now, there is one bad thing which can happen to all beautiful people; that is, they can become far too fond of mirrors. And I'm sorry to have to tell you that this is exactly what happened to the Narcissus Fairy. On days when no breeze ruffled its smooth, dark surface, the pond in the hollow made a perfect mirror. She could sit beside it, brushing her golden hair and admiring a perfect picture of herself, framed by the lacy pattern of the flowers blooming all around her.

Gradually, Narcissus spent less and less time tending her flowers and more and more time sitting by the pool gazing and smiling at her own reflection. Sometimes she hummed a little tune and sometimes she talked dreamily to herself.

"Ahhh," she would sigh, as she slowly ran a pearly comb through her hair, "doesn't my hair look lovely in the sunlight? See how it gleams. You'd think it was pure gold! And my dress must be the prettiest of all. None of the other Fairies look quite as lovely as I do."

If any of the other Flower Fairies had passed by and heard this they would have seen at once that Narcissus was falling in love with herself, but they were all much too busy to notice what was happening. They have such a lot of work to do in spring! The plants are waking up after their deep winter sleep. Tender new green leaves are beginning to uncurl and need to be protected from bad weather. In trees and bushes birds are building their nests and the Flower Fairies must watch over the eggs and the baby birds and protect them from harm. Sometimes a warm day early in spring makes hedgehogs and dormice wake too early from their winter slumbers and the Fairies have to hurry to tuck them up again before they catch a chill. So it is not surprising that the Narcissus Fairy's neglect of her duties went unnoticed.

Meanwhile, the poor narcissus flowers were beginning to look very sad. Their petals were becoming crumpled and torn and some of their leaves were withering and turning brown. A roving slug had even strayed into the hollow and seen what was happening. He quickly slithered off to tell his friends, "Come on, boys, there are some lovely juicy bulbs down there, and no one seems to be looking after them! What a feast we can have!" His friends needed no further encouragement.

The owners of the garden were very sad when they came to visit the hollow, expecting it to look as beautiful as it usually did at this time of year. "Whatever has happened this year?" they murmured sadly to one another. "We can't understand why the flowers look so unhappy." Of course, they never caught sight of the Fairy. Not even she would break the Flower Fairies' strictest rule — never to allow themselves to be seen by human beings. When she heard their footsteps approaching, she darted into a safe hiding place, under the root of a tree.

As soon as the humans had gone away again Narcissus crept back to her favourite spot at the water's edge to admire her reflection once again. At that moment a lively group of blue tits flew into the hollow to perch in the branches of the trees. Their bright little eyes never missed anything that happened in this garden, and as soon as they saw Narcissus and her poor, abandoned flowers they understood what had happened.

"Dear, dear, this will never do!" twittered the oldest and cleverest of the blue tits. "We must go and tell the rest of the Fairies at once!"

Quickly they flew away, all in different directions, and if you had been watching the garden at that moment you would have seen them darting in and out of the trees and hopping in and out of the flowerbeds as they spread the news to all the Flower Fairies.

When the Fairies arrived at the hollow they gasped with horror at what they saw.

"How could Narcissus have let this happen?" cried Guelder Rose.

"I do hope we are not too late to rescue the poor, poor flowers!" exclaimed Lavender.

Narcissus did not even notice that they were there. She was far too busy rearranging her pretty ruffled collar, to see it if looked better this way or that. Whatever could they do to attract her attention? There was only one thing they could do. Somehow they had to stop her looking at herself. They all held hands and flew over the pool, then hovered just in front of Narcissus, completely blocking out her reflection in the water.

At first a look of annoyance passed over Narcissus's face, but then she saw how anxiously her friends were looking at her. As if waking from a dream she stared at them, then blinked, then looked around, and then gasped in horror just as they had done.

"What has happened to my dear flowers?" she cried. Her friends all gathered round and told her all about her strange behaviour. She was so upset and so ashamed of herself that she burst into tears. The other Fairies did what they could to comfort her. "We'll help you put everything right, " they said.

Soon they were all bustling round, soothing and tending the sickliest flowers, and helping them to look beautiful and smell fragrant again. Two of the Fairies sternly told the slugs to go away, which they grumpily did, muttering complaints under their breath, and all the while the blue tits kept watch over the hollow to warn the busy Fairies if any humans came near. They worked until well after dusk.

Next morning a tired but happy Narcissus Fairy flew round the hollow, and saw that it was now as beautiful as it had ever been, and as the dappled sunlight sparkled on the water of the pool the first butterfly of spring flitted over the lovely Narcissus flowers.

Paint~A~Picture

With your paints, crayons, pencils or felt tips, colour the picture below using the picture on the right as a guide.

The WILD CHERRY BLOSSOM Fairy

The Song of
The Blackthorn Fairy

The wind is cold, the Spring seems long
    a-waking;
    The woods are brown and bare;
Yet this is March: soon April will be making
    All things most sweet and fair.

See, even now, in hedge and thicket tangled,
    One brave and cheering sight:
The leafless branches of the Blackthorn,
    spangled
    With starry blossoms white!

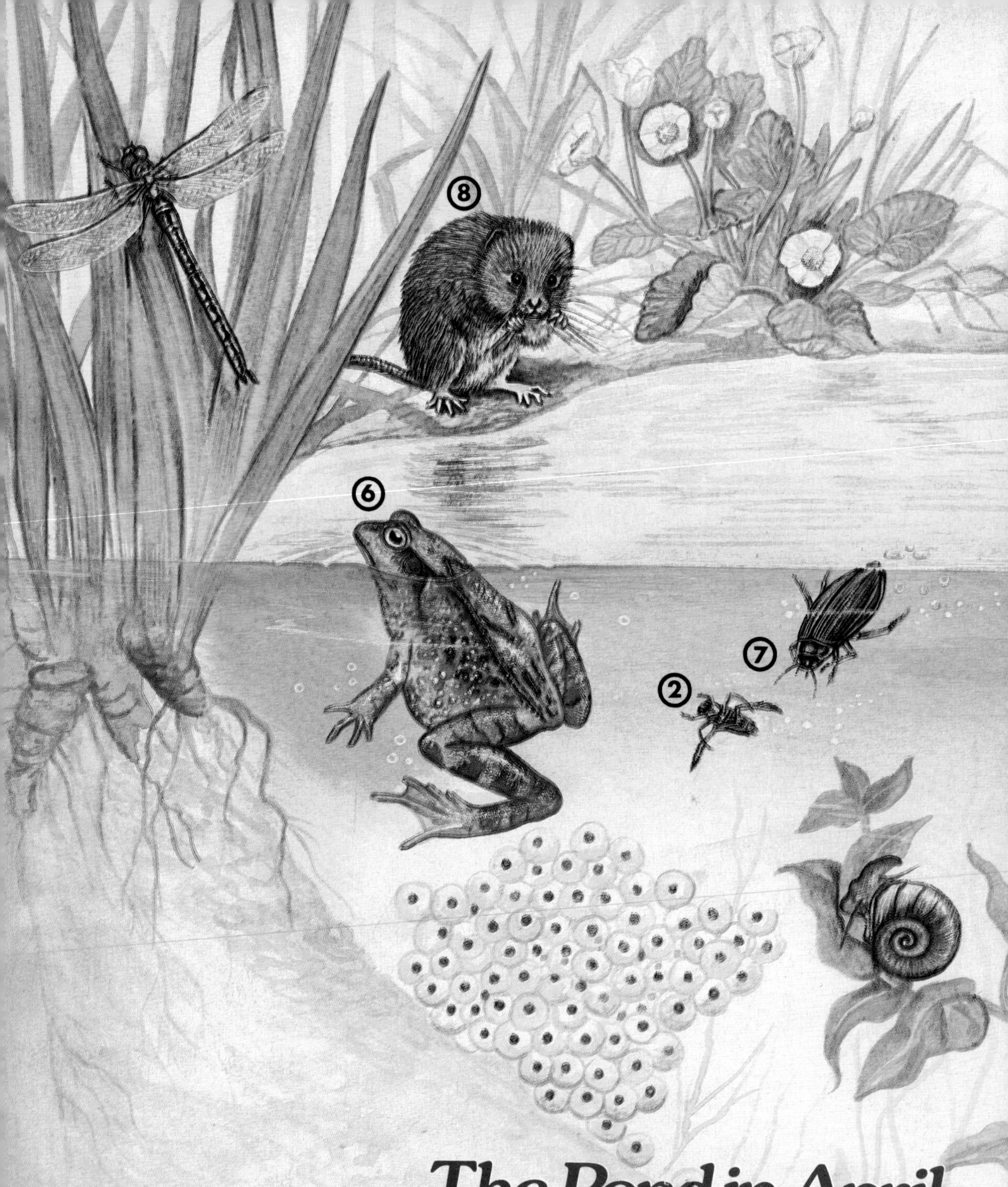

The Pond in April

It is April. The water of the pond is teeming with new life. In March, frogs gathered here and laid their eggs — or spawn — and in a few weeks time thousands of tiny tadpoles will be hatched.

The ducklings have just hatched in their nests near the water's edge, and now their mother leads them out into the water for their first swim. At this age they look like fragile bundles of brown and yellow fluff, but the mother duck keeps careful watch over them. There always seems to be one that tries to stray!

At the bottom of the pond the male stickleback has built a nest from fragments of water plants, bound together with sticky threads. He entices a female into the nest to lay her eggs. He will protect and guard the eggs and look after the young fish when they hatch.

At the edge of the water the yellow iris will soon be in flower, followed by meadowsweet with its creamy white flowers and sweet scent, and the delicate blue water forget-me-not.

1. The mallard is the most common of the dabbling ducks, which feed on water plants on or just below the surface. The drake's plumage is much more colourful than that of the mother duck.
2. The water boatman swims upside down, using his third pair of legs like oars to propel himself along. When he dives to the bottom of the pond he carries a bubble of air with him.
3. The water skater is so light that he can walk across the water. His legs just dimple the surface.
4. The male stickleback's throat and tummy have turned red, to attract a female to his nest.
5. Newts live on the land for most of the year, but in spring they come into the pond to feed and lay their eggs. The baby newts look rather like tadpoles.
6. The female frog can lay as many as three thousand eggs, called frog-spawn. Tadpoles will hatch from them in May, and when these have become fully-formed baby frogs they will leave the pond.
7. The great diving beetle floats to the surface and sticks its tail out of the water to draw in air when it needs to breathe.
8. The water vole sits on the bank washing its face after an underwater swim.

DICK TWINNEY

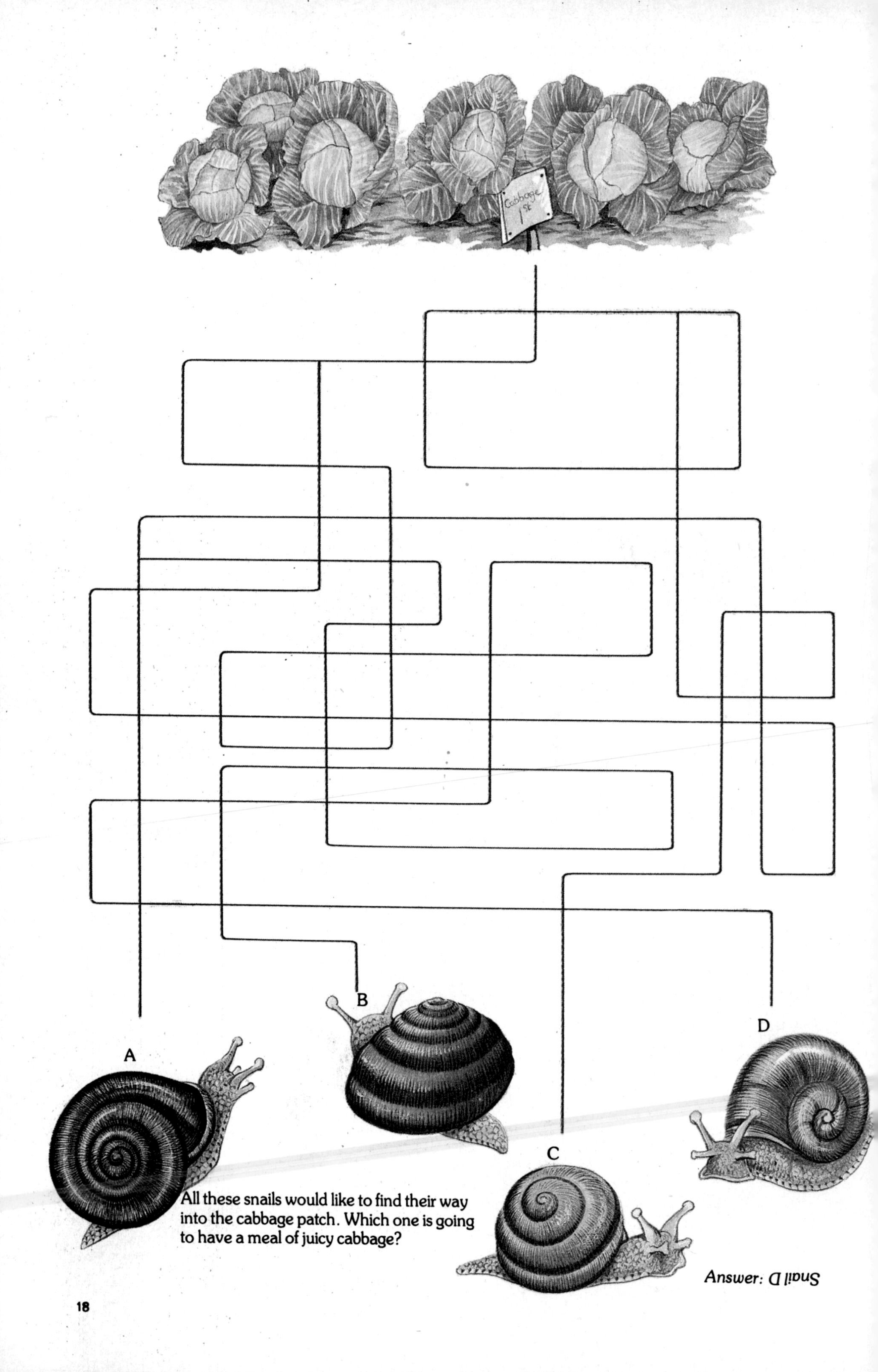

All these snails would like to find their way into the cabbage patch. Which one is going to have a meal of juicy cabbage?

Answer: Snail D

Answers: 1. FORGET-ME-NOT, 2. COWSLIP, 3. CELANDINE, 4. VIOLET, 5. PRIMROSE, 6. SNOWDROP.

Summer

The Rose Fairy and The Midsummer Ball

The Rose Fairy is the Flower Fairies' favourite little sister, with her golden curls, her chubby cheeks and her smiling face. She is as sweet-natured as you would expect the companion of the loveliest flower in the garden to be.

The story I am going to tell you about little Rose begins on Midsummer's Day. It's always a very busy and exciting day for the Flower Fairies, as they prepare for the Midsummer Ball, the grandest and most enchanting event in the whole of their year, and one that is attended by the Fairy Queen herself. The Fairies would all hate to miss it. This year, Rose was to be allowed to go to the Ball for the very first time!

You can imagine how much work there was for the Fairies to do that day: cooking and cleaning and decorating, dresses to wash, shoes to polish, tables to be set, dances to be practised and a hundred other things. But Rose was too young to help the other Fairies.

"You just rest quietly here in the rose bush," they said, "and don't get tired. It's going to be a very long day for you today, and you won't get to bed until very late." With that they flew away to check that the grasshopper band had learned all their tunes properly, and to see whether the fireflies had gathered in the trees around the fairy dell, ready to light the Fairy Queen's path to the Ball.

Rose tried very hard to sit still for a while, but she found this very dull. It's difficult to sit still when you're feeling excited about going to your first Ball! So she was delighted when her friends the elves arrived and announced that they'd come to play with her. They had been trying to help prepare for the Ball, carrying little mushroom tables and chairs to set around the dance floor, but they kept dropping things and falling over, and got into such a muddle that the Fairies had to tell them to stop trying to be helpful and go somewhere else where they couldn't cause any more trouble!

The elves, like everyone else, were very fond of Rose. They loved the way her face dimpled into a smile when she saw them, and liked the sound of her merry laugh when they told her silly jokes. She never seemed to mind, either, if they got the jokes wrong, or forgot the last line.

"Come and tell me some stories," pleaded Rose. "I'm supposed to be having a rest, but it's so boring sitting here all by myself!"

The elves perched all around her in the rose bush, and one by one tried to think of stories to tell her. But they didn't really know very many, and after a while even storytelling seemed rather dull. The elves were no better at sitting still than Rose, to tell the truth.

"I know, let's play hide-and-seek instead," said Plantain. "Rose can hide first, and we'll all look for her."

So all the elves climbed out of the rose bush and stood below it with their eyes tight shut, counting slowly, "One . . . two . . . three . . . " Rose looked round quickly for somewhere to hide and saw one lovely big bloom at the top of the bush, with its petals curling over in the middle to make the perfect hiding place. She crept in and curled up as small as she could.

" . . . ninety-nine, one hundred — coming!" shouted the elves, clambering energetically back into the bush. They looked under leaves, peeped round buds, peered into nearby bushes, but they couldn't see Rose anywhere.

"I know where she is," yelled Thistle, finally. "Look at the way that flower is shaking! I bet she's in there. She's got the giggles and can't keep still!" He was quite right, and the flower shook even more when Rose heard him.

With a yelp of triumph Thistle leapt at the flower, rocking it so violently that poor Rose came tumbling out, bounced off a branch and caught her pretty pink dress on a thorn. There was a horrible tearing noise as the fabric ripped and she fell once again, landing on the ground with quite a bump.

She was very brave about the fall, and said that she wasn't hurt at all, but when she looked down and saw what had happened to her dress she couldn't hold back her tears any longer. How could she go to the Ball with a torn dress? She would have to stay at home after all. What a disappointment!

The elves were miserable too. They hadn't meant anything like this to happen and they felt it was all their fault. Then Privet remembered seeing a sign outside Granny Spider's house. "Dressmaking, tailoring, alterations and INVISIBLE MENDING," it said. So they decided to take the dress there at once.

Rose crept back into her flower, passed her dress out to them and then pulled the petals round her to keep herself warm, while the elves hurried off to Granny Spider's house and rang her bell. Granny Spider came out looking rather grumpy and muttering that they'd woken her from her afternoon nap, but when she saw what had happened to dear little Rose's dress she stopped grumbling and agreed at once to mend it.

"Just leave it to me, my dears," she said.

She spun lengths and lengths of fine, silky threads and wove them in and out of the dress so quickly that the elves felt quite dizzy just watching her eight legs plying back and forth. In no time at all the dress was mended so perfectly that you would never have known it had been damaged.

The elves hurried back to where Rose was waiting anxiously. It was nearly dusk and she had just enough time to put the dress on before the other Fairies arrived to take her to the Ball. When they heard what had happened, and how upset she had been they said that she could have the best seat at the Ball to watch the moonlight ballet they were to perform in honour of the Fairy Queen.

It was a magical evening. The fireflies glittered in the trees; the grasshopper band played beautifully, and the ballet was the loveliest sight that Rose had ever seen, with a broad beam of moonlight shining on the centre of the dance floor like a silvery spotlight. Best of all, the Fairy Queen stopped on her way to her throne and spoke to Rose, who blushed as pink as her dress and quite forgot the curtsey she had been practising for weeks beforehand.

"This was the best day ever," murmured Rose. Then she fell fast asleep on her mushroom and her Fairy sisters carried her home to bed.

Paint~A~Picture

With your paints, crayons, pencils or felt tips, colour the picture below using the picture on the right as a guide.

The CANTERBURY BELL Fairy

The Song of
The Poppy Fairy

The green wheat's a-growing,
    The lark sings on high;
In scarlet silk-a-glowing,
    Here stand I.

The wheat's turning yellow,
    Ripening for sheaves;
I hear the little fellow
    Who scares the bird-thieves.

Now the harvest's ended,
    The wheat-field is bare;
But still, red and splendid,
    I am there.

CMB

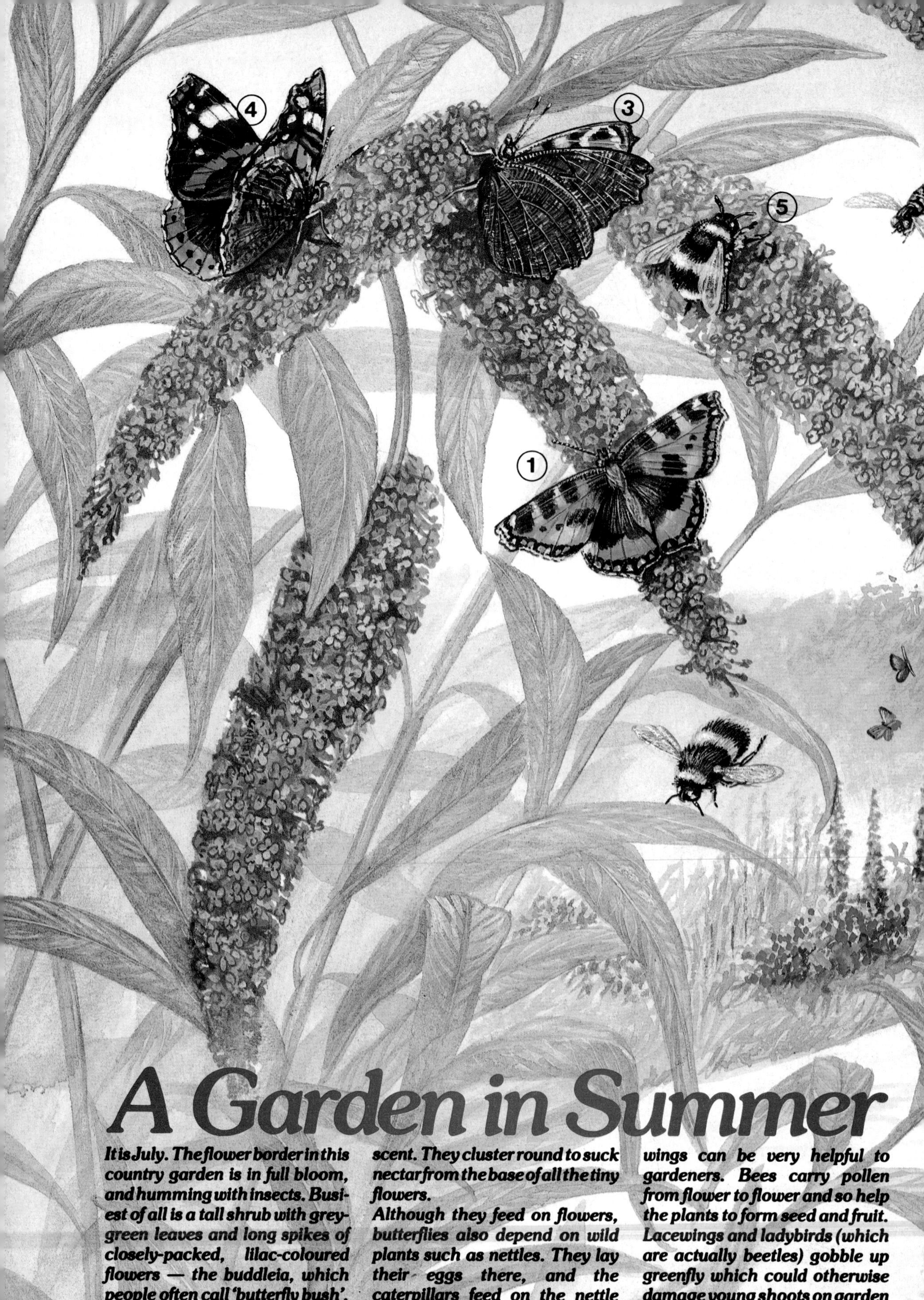

A Garden in Summer

It is July. The flower border in this country garden is in full bloom, and humming with insects. Busiest of all is a tall shrub with grey-green leaves and long spikes of closely-packed, lilac-coloured flowers — the buddleia, which people often call 'butterfly bush'. Butterflies, bees and hover-flies are all attracted by its sweet scent. They cluster round to suck nectar from the base of all the tiny flowers.

Although they feed on flowers, butterflies also depend on wild plants such as nettles. They lay their eggs there, and the caterpillars feed on the nettle leaves.

Insects such as bees and lacewings can be very helpful to gardeners. Bees carry pollen from flower to flower and so help the plants to form seed and fruit. Lacewings and ladybirds (which are actually beetles) gobble up greenfly which could otherwise damage young shoots on garden plants by sucking their sap.

1. The Small Tortoiseshell is one of the butterflies most often seen in gardens. The caterpillars feed on nettles.

2. The Peacock butterfly's wings have 'eye' markings like the pattern on a peacock's tail. When attacked by a bird, the butterfly opens its wings to reveal the 'eyes' and frighten the bird away.

3. Butterflies normally rest with their wings together, showing only the dull-coloured undersides.

4. Red Admirals fly to this country every spring from lands around the Mediterranean Sea. They also lay their eggs on nettles.

5. The bumblebee collects pollen from garden flowers and carries it back to the nest in special sacs on its legs.

6. The ladybird's hard, red, spotted wing cases conceal a pair of wings with which it can 'fly away home'. This is the seven-spot ladybird.

7. The Large White butterfly is unpopular with gardeners because its caterpillars sometimes eat cabbages.

Can you name these butterflies? Answers at the bottom of the page.

Answers: 1. Orange Tip, 2. Red Admiral, 3. Small Tortoiseshell, 4. Peacock, 5. Swallowtail, 6. Comma.

The Box Tree Fairy wants to go to the far corner of the garden to read the sundial, but he can only travel along the box hedges. Can you find the way for him?

Autumn

The Hazelnut Fairy and The Elves

At the foot of an old oak tree, right in the middle of the wood, is the school where the elves have their lessons. As well as reading, writing and arithmetic they learn all about the weather, the changing seasons and how to care for plants. Their schoolteacher is an old, rather grumpy, but extremely wise owl. He is a good teacher because he knows as much as you could ever wish to know about all sorts of things, but he is also very strict. His sharp eyes never fail to notice any elf who isn't paying attention, or is trying to pass notes, or flick ink pellets with his ruler or any of the other things you shouldn't do in class. Even when his back is turned and he is writing on the blackboard, the elves know they'd better behave themselves, because the owl can turn his head right round on his shoulders to glare sternly at any young elf who has dared to whisper, or shuffle his books about, or drop his pencil.

Usually, the elves don't mind behaving themselves because they know that every now and then they are going to get a chance to be a little bit naughty. You see, their teacher has one big problem: sometimes he finds it difficult to keep his eyes open. He is really a night bird, and it's hard to stay awake all day when you've been on the wing all night. So, when the elves notice him slowly blinking, and see his eyelids start to droop they know that soon they will be free to do whatever they want.

One bright autumn day when the elves were in the middle of a particularly boring lesson — learning the Latin names of plants by heart — Mr. Owl suddenly drifted off in the middle of a sentence into a deep sleep. It was the first sunny day after weeks of miserable wet, windy weather, and the elves would

much rather have been out in the wood searching for conkers or clambering in the trees and bushes, picking nuts and berries. So as soon as they were sure that the owl was fast asleep they tiptoed out of the classroom and escaped into the fresh air.

Before long they were up to all sorts of mischief! The Horse Chestnut Elf slithered along a branch of his tree and started dropping conkers onto any unsuspecting animal who happened to walk past. (Luckily he didn't hit anybody, but the animals got quite a shock when the prickly green conker cases came hurtling down and burst at their feet!) Pine Tree and Privet were bombarding each other with pine cones, shouting and yelling as they did so. And Plantain was standing whistling, his hands in his pockets, trying to pretend that he hadn't *really* taken Thistle's lunch box and hidden it under a bush!

In another part of the wood, not far away, the Hazelnut Fairy was busy checking to see if the nuts on her tree were ripe and ready for people or animals to pick. When she heard the dreadful commotion the elves were making, she hurried off to find out what they were doing and why they were not at school.

On her way there she met Mrs. Squirrel, who was running backwards and forwards under the trees, scuffling about in piles of leaves and muttering to herself: "Oh dear, oh dear. Whatever shall I do? Where can they be? How am I going to feed my little ones?"

Hazelnut gently took her by the hand. "Whatever is the matter, Mrs. Squirrel?" she said.

"I don't know how I can be so silly!" said Mrs. Squirrel, giving a little sniff and wiping away a tear. "But I do this every year! I gather all the nuts I need to feed the family right through the winter, and then I forget where I've buried them. I thought I'd remember this time, but now the wind has brought down all these leaves and everything looks different. I'll never find them now!"

Hazelnut took a dainty handkerchief from her pocket and helped Mrs. Squirrel to dry her tears. "There, there," she said. "I'm sure I can help you. The nuts on my tree are just ready to be picked. But first we'd better find out what those naughty elves are doing."

By this time the elves had started a football match. Half of them were kicking a large conker back and forth between two sets of twiggy goalposts and the rest were jumping up and down on the sidelines yelling encouragement to the players. The noise was dreadful! Hazelnut had to clap her hands and shout rather loud to make them hear.

Of course, the elves had no real excuse for not being at school, and they were very embarrassed at being found out.

"Never mind," said Hazelnut. "I won't tell your teacher, but perhaps you can do something good and kind to make up for being such naughty boys. Poor Mrs. Squirrel has lost all her winter stores. There are plenty of nuts on my tree. Will you come along and help me pick them for her?"

"Oh, yes!" they all said, eagerly. Soon they were hard at work. Some were in the Hazel tree picking the nuts and throwing them down. Some stood below to catch the nuts and others stacked them in neat little piles.

"Oh thank you, thank you," said Mrs. Squirrel. "You are so kind!"

Meanwhile, back at the school, Mr. Owl was waking up. When he saw the empty classroom he didn't know whether to be angrier with himself for going to sleep in class or with the elves for taking advantage of his little nap! But he was in a very bad mood as he flew over the treetops in search of his missing pupils.

Owls fly so quietly that no one heard the teacher coming and they got quite a fright when he swooped down beside the Hazel tree. He was just about to tell the elves how severely he was going to punish them when the Hazelnut Fairy darted forward.

"Please don't be too angry with them, Mr. Owl," she pleaded. "I know they have been very naughty boys, but they've been so kind and helpful to Mrs. Squirrel that you must forgive them!"

"Oh yes, I don't know how I would have managed without their help," said Mrs. Squirrel, giving a little curtsey, because she was secretly rather nervous of Mr. Owl.

It was hard for the owl to be angry with the elves when he saw how hard they had been working and heard the rest of the story from Mrs. Squirrel and Hazelnut. So he decided to forgive them just this once.

"But don't ever run away from school again," he added gruffly.

Then Mrs. Squirrel invited them all back to her house for tea, and the Fairy brought some lovely hazelnut meringues for them to eat, and by the time everyone was ready to go home they were tired, happy and very full up. And the elves promised to try to be good at school all of the next day. Do you think they really were?

Paint~A~Picture

With your paints, crayons, pencils or felt tips, colour the picture below using the picture on the right as a guide.

The MICHAELMAS DAISY Fairy

The Song of
The Blackberry Fairy

My berries cluster black and thick
For rich and poor alike to pick.

I'll tear your dress, and cling, and tease,
And scratch your hands and arms and
knees.

I'll stain your fingers and your face,
And then I'll laugh at your disgrace.

But when the bramble-jelly's made,
You'll find your trouble well repaid.

MB

The Hedgerow in September

It is September. In the hedgerow blackberries, rose hips and hawthorn berries are ripening. The leaves on the brambles are beginning to turn from green to gold and red.

All through the year, the hedgerow has provided shelter for small creatures who are too timid to venture out into the open: wood mice, bank voles and hedgehogs. Birds built their nests here in spring and reared their young in the protection of the bushy hawthorn twigs. Mice and voles burrowed into the bank below. Now, in the autumn, the dog rose, blackthorn and bramble offer food to the birds, insects and small mammals.

This hedge may have been planted in the eighteenth century, when many of our fields were first enclosed. At first, it would have been a row of young hawthorn bushes. As they grew, their branches were bent over and woven around upright stakes. Later, seeds from blackberries, rose hips and blackthorn were dropped by birds, and fluffy seeds from the traveller's joy were carried here by the wind to take root amongst the hawthorn.

1. Hedgehogs come out at dusk to feed on insects, worms and grubs. They build nests of leaves and grass in the hedgerow, to raise their babies in, and for their winter sleep.
2. Woodmice tunnel into the banks below hedges, to make their nests. In the autumn they climb into the hedge to feed on hawthorn berries and rose hips.
3. Tiny wrens sometimes build their nests in hedges. When frightened they fly into the hedge to hide.
4. Blackbirds love to eat blackberries, but they spit out the seeds.
5. The Red Admiral butterfly sucks juice from ripe blackberries through her long hollow tongue. In the spring she laid her eggs on the nettles below the hedge.
6. Spiders spin their webs among the brambles, to catch the insects who come to feed on the sticky blackberry juice. On misty autumn mornings their lacy webs are hung with dew-drops.
7. Hawthorn is the plant most often found in hedgerows. In May it bears creamy white flowers (provided that the hedge has not been trimmed back too hard) and now, in September, its berries are ripening. Many birds and animals will feed on them during the winter.
8. Brambles provide food not just for humans, but for many birds and insects.
9. The dog rose brightens the hedge-rows with its flowers in June and July, and its bright red fruits in autumn. The rose hips can be made into a syrup rich in vitamin C.
10. As the seeds of the traveller's joy ripen, they develop fluffy white hairs which will help the wind to carry them away. So, in autumn, this plant is called Old Man's Beard.
11. The blackthorn's bitter fruits, sloes, can be made into a jelly or used to flavour gin.

Can you name all the animals in this wood? Give yourself 4 points for a correct answer, and 2 if you were half right. Then check your score at the bottom of the page.

1. Pine Marten, 2. Red Deer, 3. Fox, 4. Grey Squirrel, 5. Heath Snail, 6. Toad, 7. Hedgehog, 8. Small Tortoiseshell Butterfly, 9. Badger, 10. Rabbits, 11 Green Woodpecker.

Score: 44 Super Nature Spotter
32-44 Good
24-32 Still Learning
Below 24 Lots to Learn

11
10
7
9
8

Winter

The Christmas Tree Fairy

It was the week before Christmas. Amanda and Jane, aged eight and ten, had just been tucked up in bed by their mother, and in the tiny bedroom next door their baby brother was fast asleep with one arm round a battered old teddy bear and one thumb stuck firmly in his mouth.

Neither of the two girls felt the least bit like going to sleep, however. Today had been the last day of term; Christmas had nearly come, and they could think of nothing else. They talked in excited whispers about all the good things that were going to happen, the presents they were hoping for, the decorations, the tree . . .

"And Dad will come home," murmured Amanda, just before she finally fell asleep.

Downstairs in the kitchen her mother was worrying about how to make this Christmas as much fun for the family as it had been last year.

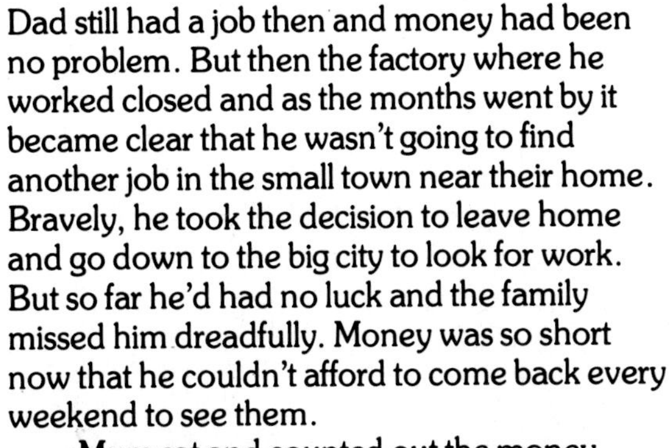

Dad still had a job then and money had been no problem. But then the factory where he worked closed and as the months went by it became clear that he wasn't going to find another job in the small town near their home. Bravely, he took the decision to leave home and go down to the big city to look for work. But so far he'd had no luck and the family missed him dreadfully. Money was so short now that he couldn't afford to come back every weekend to see them.

Mum sat and counted out the money she'd managed to put by for presents for the children. It wasn't much. She hoped they hadn't set their hearts on any really expensive toys.

The next morning, when breakfast was over and Mum had cleaned up the baby — who as usual seemed to have got more food on him than in him — she suggested they should spend the day putting up the Christmas decorations. Jane wrapped the baby warmly in his outdoor clothes and sat him in his pushchair while Amanda helped Mum to fetch their old pram from the garden shed. They were going to use it to carry evergreens back from the wood near their house.

The pram was soon full of trailing ivy and prickly holly, bright with red berries, and they spent the rest of the morning arranging it across mantelpieces, on top of pictures and along shelves. Their hands were quite sore by lunchtime where the holly had pricked them.

After lunch, when the baby had settled down for his afternoon nap, Mum said, "Let's bring the tree in now." They didn't need to buy one, because they had bought a growing tree a few years ago, and each year they planted it again carefully in the garden when Christmas was over.

Mum dug up the tree and put it into a tub and Jane and Amanda gently pressed the earth down around its roots. Carrying it indoors was quite difficult, because the earth in the tub made it so heavy, but at last they managed to set it up by the sitting room window. Mum brought down a box of glass balls and garlands from the attic, and by tea time the tree looked beautiful with all its decorations. Only the top of the tree looked strangely bare, as if something was missing.

"I wish we had a fairy for our tree," sighed Jane.

The next day they took the bus to town to do their Christmas shopping. Mum had given both of the girls a little money to buy presents for each other and the baby, and halfway through the morning she was going to leave them at the library to listen to stories while she slipped away to buy presents for them.

First they went into the big store in the middle of town, and as they struggled through the crowded, bustling department selling Christmas decorations Amanda suddenly stopped and tugged her mother's sleeve.

"Mum, look!" she cried. "Isn't she beautiful! Oh, please can we buy her!"

She was looking at a lovely fairy doll with golden hair and a white dress with layers of lacy petticoats. There was a star on her forehead and a silver wand in her hand. She would look perfect at the top of their tree.

For a moment they all stopped and stared at the fairy doll. Then Mum picked her up in her tissue-lined box and looked at the price label. She put the box down again quickly.

"No, I'm sorry," she said hastily and walked away, pushing the pushchair with one hand and pulling Amanda away with the other. She was afraid this was going to be the first of many disappointments for the children today, and didn't want to linger over it.

The following day was Christmas Eve. Mum was busy cooking and baking all day and the girls had the job of entertaining the baby and keeping him out of Mum's way. When evening came, Amanda and Jane pressed their noses to the window of the front room, eager to see Dad the moment he walked through the front gate.

At last the gate opened and a weary, sad looking figure came up the garden path. The girls threw open the door and flung their arms

round their father as he stood blinking in the light spilling out from the hall. For a few moments no one could make themselves heard as the girls chattered away, trying to tell Dad everything all at once. Then at last Mum, who had come out of the kitchen, had a chance to speak to him.

He hadn't any good news to tell her. There were no jobs to be found. Maybe things would get better in the New Year, he said, without much hope in his voice.

There was a strange look on Mum's face as she pulled an envelope from the pocket of her apron. All day she'd been keeping a secret from the family and now the moment had come to tell them about it. She explained, rather shyly, that she had applied for a job as a teacher at the local school. She hadn't expected to get it. After all, it was more than ten years since she had left her last job, but apparently her old headmistress had given her an excellent reference and the school had offered her the job. Their letter must have been delayed in the Christmas mail. It had only come that morning — in the very last delivery before Christmas!

Dad looked as if he didn't know whether to laugh or cry. He hugged Mum.

"At least you'll be able to stay home now," she said, "and maybe there will be a job for you after Christmas, not so far away."

That night when the tired but happy family had gone to bed, something magical happened. The little Christmas tree had a guardian — the real Christmas Tree Fairy. The family had never seen her, but she knew all about them and had felt sorry for them through all their troubles. Now she knew that there was only one thing missing to make their Christmas joy complete. Silently she slipped through a skylight window and flitted down to the sitting room where she took her place at the top of the tree and stood there, perfectly still, just like a doll.

When the family came downstairs the next morning they couldn't believe their eyes. All they knew was that something miraculous had happened. And they felt sure that this meant their luck was going to change from now on.

"Now I know this is going to be the best Christmas we've ever had," whispered Amanda.

Paint~A~Picture

With your paints, crayons, pencils or felt tips, colour the picture below using the picture on the right as a guide.

The WINTER JASMINE Fairy

The Song of The Holly Fairy

O, I am green in Winter-time,
When other trees are brown;
Of all the trees (So saith the rhyme)
The holly bears the crown.
December days are drawing near
When I shall come to town,
And carol-boys go singing clear
Of all the trees (O hush and hear!)
The holly bears the crown!

For who so well-beloved and merry
As the scarlet Holly Berry?

CMB

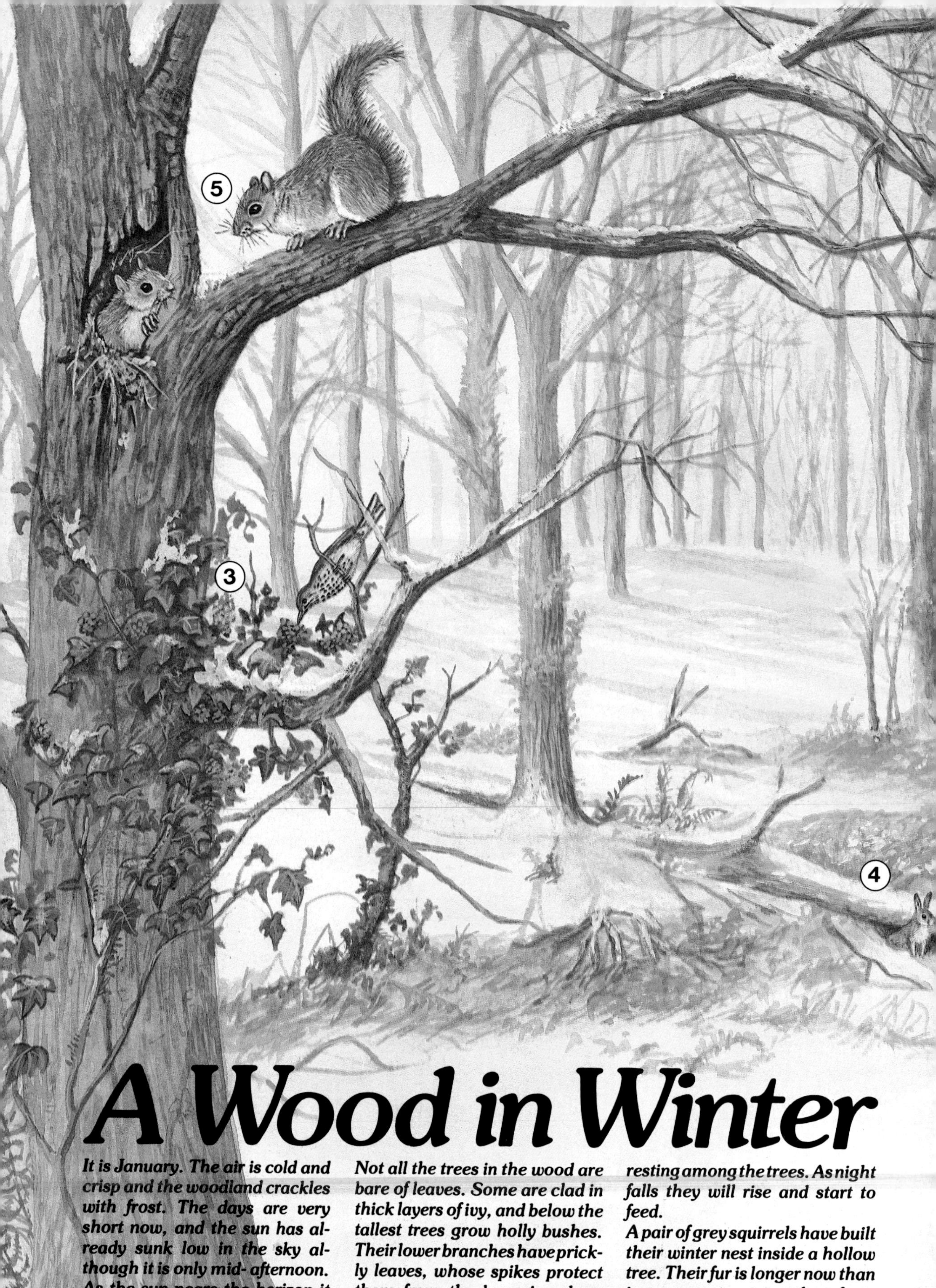

A Wood in Winter

It is January. The air is cold and crisp and the woodland crackles with frost. The days are very short now, and the sun has already sunk low in the sky although it is only mid- afternoon. As the sun nears the horizon it seems to grow larger and larger, and it casts a rosy glow over the western sky. The bare branches of the woodland trees are silhouetted against the glow.

Not all the trees in the wood are bare of leaves. Some are clad in thick layers of ivy, and below the tallest trees grow holly bushes. Their lower branches have prickly leaves, whose spikes protect them from the browsing deer. Some of the bushes bear bright red berries — food for wood pigeons, starlings and thrushes. A herd of shy fallow deer has taken shelter in the wood and is resting among the trees. As night falls they will rise and start to feed.

A pair of grey squirrels have built their winter nest inside a hollow tree. Their fur is longer now than in summer, to protect them from the cold. Out of sight, other small animals are hibernating — in a deep sleep until the warmer weather comes.

1. Fallow deer herd together in the winter. In the summer the bucks and does live apart.

2. The holly's leaves are dark, glossy and tough. Some of the bushes are male and the others female. Only the females bear berries. People have used holly to decorate their homes in midwinter for hundreds of years — even before Christmas was first celebrated.

3. Ivy flowers in the autumn and bears berries in the spring, unlike most other plants. Like the holly it is evergreen.

4. Fallen trees provide homes and food for many different animals and for plants such as moss and fungi.

5. Grey squirrels came to this country from America at the end of the nineteenth century and are now more common than our own red squirrels.

6. The woodland floor is carpeted with dead leaves. Because so little sunlight can reach down here, few plants grow beneath the trees.

All these animals have left their footprints in the snow. Can you tell which animal made which tracks?
1
2
3
4
5
A *red deer*
B *hare*
E *squirrel*
D *fox*
C *badger*
Answers: A – 2, B – 3, C – 4, D – 5, E – 1

Who lives where? See if you can guess.
Then follow the lines to find the answers.
badger
fox
dormouse
hedgehog
squirrel